The Dressmaker's Child

WILLIAM TREVOR

PENGUIN BOOKS

PENGUIN BOOKS

Published by the Penguin Group
Penguin Books Ltd, 80 Strand, London WC2R 0RL, England
Penguin Group (USA) Inc., 375 Hudson Street, New York, New York 10014, USA
Penguin Group (Canada), 10 Alcorn Avenue, Toronto, Ontario, Canada M4V 3B2
(a division of Pearson Penguin Canada Inc.)
Penguin Ireland, 25 St Stephen's Green, Dublin 2, Ireland
(a division of Penguin Books Ltd)
Penguin Group (Australia), 250 Camberwell Road, Camberwell, Victoria 3124,
Australia (a division of Pearson Australia Group Pty Ltd)
Penguin Books India Pvt Ltd, 11 Community Centre,
Panchsheel Park, New Delhi – 110 017, India
Penguin Group (NZ), cnr Airborne and Rosedale Roads, Albany,
Auckland 1310, New Zealand (a division of Pearson New Zealand Ltd)
Penguin Books (South Africa) (Pty) Ltd, 24 Sturdee Avenue,
Rosebank 2196, South Africa

Penguin Books Ltd, Registered Offices: 80 Strand, London WC2R 0RL, England

www.penguin.com

'The Piano Tuner's Wives' first published in *After Rain*, Viking 1996
'The Hill Bachelors' first published in *The Hill Bachelors*, Viking 2000
'The Dressmaker's Child' first published in *The New Yorker* magazine 2005
This selection published as a Pocket Penguin 2005
1

Grateful acknowledgement is made to Random House Canada for permission to reprint 'The Piano Tuner's Wives' and 'The Hill Bachelors'

Set in 10.5/12.5pt Monotype Dante
Typeset by Palimpsest Book Production Limited
Polmont, Stirlingshire
Printed in England by Clays Ltd, St Ives plc

Contents

The Dressmaker's Child

Cahal sprayed WD-40 on to the only bolt his spanner wouldn't shift. All the others had come out easily enough but this one was rusted in, the exhaust unit trailing from it. He had tried to hammer it out, he had tried wrenching the exhaust unit this way and that in the hope that something would give way, but nothing had. Half five, he'd told Heslin, and the bloody car wouldn't be ready.

The lights of the garage were always on because shelves had been put up in front of the windows that stretched across the length of the wall at the back. Abandoned cars, kept for their parts, and cars and motor-cycles waiting for spares, and jacks that could be wheeled about, took up what space there was on either side of the small wooden office, which was at the back also. There were racks of tools, and workbenches with vices along the back wall, and rows of new and reconditioned tyres, and drums of grease and oil. In the middle of the garage there were two pits, in one of which Cahal's father was at the moment, putting in a clutch. There was a radio on which advice was being given about looking after fish in an aquarium. 'Will you turn that stuff off?' Cahal's father shouted from under the car he was working on, and Cahal searched the wavebands until he found music of his father's time.

He was an only son in a family of girls, all of them older, all of them gone from the town – three to England, another in Dunne's in Galway, another married in Nebraska. The garage was what Cahal knew, having kept his father company there since childhood, given odd jobs to do as he grew up. His father had had help then, an old man who was related to the family, whose place Cahal eventually took.

He tried the bolt again but the WD-40 hadn't begun to work yet. He was a lean, almost scrawny youth, dark-haired, his long face usually unsmiling. His garage overalls, over a yellow T-shirt, were oil-stained, gone pale where their green dye had been washed out of them. He was nineteen years old.

'Hullo,' a voice said. A man and a woman, strangers, stood in the wide-open doorway of the garage.

'Howya,' Cahal said.

'It's the possibility, sir,' the man enquired, 'you drive us to the sacred Virgin?'

'Sorry?' And Cahal's father shouted up from the pit, wanting to know who was there. 'Which Virgin's that?' Cahal asked.

The two looked at one another, not attempting to answer, and it occurred to Cahal that they were foreign people, who had not understood. A year ago a German had driven his Volkswagen into the garage, with a noise in the engine, so he'd said. 'I had hopes it'd be the big end,' Cahal's father admitted afterwards, but it was only the catch of the bonnet gone a bit loose. A couple from America had had a tyre put on their hired car a few weeks after that, but there'd been nothing since.

'Of Pouldearg,' the woman said. 'Is it how to say it?'

'The statue you're after?'

They nodded uncertainly and then with more confidence, both of them at the same time.

'Aren't you driving, yourselves, though?' Cahal asked them.

'We have no car,' the man said.

'We are travelled from Ávila.' The woman's black hair was

silky, drawn back and tied with a red-and-blue ribbon. Her eyes were brown, her teeth very white, her skin olive. She wore the untidy clothes of a traveller: denim trousers, a woollen jacket over a striped-red blouse. The man's trousers were the same, his shirt a nondescript shade of greyish blue, a white kerchief at his neck. A few years older than himself, Cahal estimated they'd be.

'Ávila?' he said.

'Spain,' the man said.

Again Cahal's father called out, and Cahal said two Spanish people had come into the garage.

'In the store,' the man explained. 'They say you drive us to the Virgin.'

'Are they broken down?' Cahal's father shouted.

He could charge them fifty euros, Pouldearg there and back, Cahal considered. He'd miss Germany versus Holland on the television, maybe the best match of the Cup, but never mind that for fifty euros.

'The only thing,' he said, 'I have an exhaust to put in.'

He pointed at the pipe and silencer hanging out of Heslin's old Vauxhall, and they understood. He gestured with his hands that they should stay where they were for a minute, and with his palms held flat made a pushing motion in the air, indicating that they should ignore the agitation that was coming from the pit. Both of them were amused. When Cahal tried the bolt again it began to turn.

He made the thumbs-up sign when exhaust and silencer clattered to the ground. 'I could take you at around seven,' he said, going close to where the Spaniards stood, keeping his voice low so that his father would not hear. He led them to the forecourt and made the arrangement while he filled the tank of a Murphy's Stout lorry.

*

When Cahal's father had driven a mile out on the Bantry road, he turned at the entrance to the stud farm and drove back to the garage, satisfied that the clutch he'd put in for Father Shea was correctly adjusted. He left the car on the forecourt, ready for Father Shea to collect, and hung the keys up in the office. Heslin from the court-house was writing a cheque for the exhaust Cahal had fitted. Cahal was getting out of his overalls and when Heslin had gone he said the people who had come wanted him to drive them to Pouldearg. They were Spanish people, Cahal said again, in case his father hadn't heard when he'd supplied that information before.

'What they want with Pouldearg?'

'Nothing only the statue.'

'There's no one goes to the statue these times.'

'It's where they're headed.'

'Did you tell them, though, how the thing was?'

'I did of course.'

'Why they'd be going out there?'

'There's people takes photographs of it.'

Thirteen years ago, the then bishop and two parish priests had put an end to the cult of the wayside statue at Pouldearg. None of those three men, and no priest or nun who had ever visited the crossroads at Pouldearg, had sensed anything special about the statue; none had witnessed the tears that were said to slip out of the downcast eyes when pardon for sins was beseeched by penitents. The statue became the subject of attention in pulpits and in religious publications, the claims made for it fulminated against as a foolishness. And then a curate of that time demonstrated that what had been noticed by two or three local people who regularly passed by the statue – a certain dampness beneath the eyes – was no more than raindrops trapped in two overdefined hollows. There the matter ended. Those who had so certainly believed in what they had never actually seen, those who had not noticed the drenched leaves of overhanging boughs high above the statue, felt as foolish as their spiritual masters had predicted they one day would. Almost overnight the weeping Virgin of Pouldearg became again the painted image it had always been. Our Lady of the Wayside, it had been called for a while.

'I never heard people were taking photographs of it.' Cahal's father shook his head as if he doubted his son, which he often did and usually with reason.

'A fellow was writing a book a while back. Going around all Ireland, tracking down the weeping statues.'

'It was no more than the rain at Pouldearg.'

'He'd have put that in the book. That man would have put the whole thing down, how you'd find the statues all over the place and some of them would be okay and some of them wouldn't.'

'And you set the Spaniards right about Pouldearg?'

'I did of course.'

'Drain the juice out of young Leahy's bike and we'll weld his leak for him.'

The suspicions of Cahal's father were justified: the truth had no more than slightly played a part in what Cahal had told the Spanish couple about Pouldearg. With fifty euros at the back of his mind, he would have considered it a failure of his intelligence had he allowed himself to reveal that the miracle once claimed for the statue at Pouldearg was without foundation. They had heard the statue called Our Lady of Tears as well as Our Lady of the Wayside and the Sacred Virgin of Pouldearg by a man in a Dublin public house with whom they had drifted into conversation. They'd had to repeat this a couple of times before Cahal grasped what they were saying, but he thought he got it right in the end. It wouldn't be hard to stretch the journey by four or five miles, and if they were misled by the names they'd heard the statue given in Dublin it was no concern of his. At five past seven, when he'd had his tea and had had a look at the television, he drove into the yard of Macey's Hotel. He waited there as he'd said he would. They appeared almost at once.

They sat close together in the back. Before he started the engine again Cahal told them what the cost would be and they said that was all right. He drove through the town, gone quiet as it invariably did at this time. Some of the shops were still open and would remain so for a few more hours – the newsagents' and tobacconists', the sweet shops and small groceries, Quinlan's supermarket, all the public houses – but there was a lull on the streets.

'Are you on holiday?' Cahal asked.

He couldn't make much of their reply. Both of them spoke, correcting one another. After a lot of repetition they seemed to be telling him that they were getting married.

'Well, that's grand,' he said.

He turned out on to the Loye road. Spanish was spoken in the back of the car. The radio wasn't working or he'd have put it on for company. The car was a black Ford Cortina with a hundred and eighty thousand miles on the clock that his father had taken in part-exchange. They'd use it until the tax disc expired and then put it aside for spares. Cahal thought of telling them that in case they'd think he hadn't much to say for himself, but he knew it would be too difficult. The Christian Brothers had had him labelled as not having much to say for himself, and it had stuck in his memory, worrying him sometimes in case it caused people to believe he was slow. Whenever he could, Cahal tried to give the lie to that by making a comment.

'Are you here long?' he enquired, and the girl said they'd been two days in Dublin. He said he'd been in Dublin himself a few times. He said it was mountainy from now on, until they reached Pouldearg. The scenery was beautiful, the girl said.

He took the fork at the two dead trees, although going straight would have got them there too, longer still but potholes all over the place. It was a good car for the hills, the man said, and Cahal said it was a Ford, pleased that he'd understood. You'd get used to it, he considered, with a bit more practising you'd pick up the trick of understanding them.

'How'd you say it in Spanish,' he called back over his shoulder. 'A statue?'

'*Estatua*,' they both said, together. '*Estatua*,' they said.

'*Estatua*,' Cahal repeated, changing gear for the hill at Loye.

The girl clapped her hands, and he could see her smiling in the driving mirror. God, a woman like that, he thought. Give me a woman like that, he said to himself, and he imagined he was in the car alone with her, that the man wasn't there, that he hadn't come to Ireland with her, that he didn't exist.

'Do you hear about St Teresa of Ávila? Do you hear about her in Ireland?' Her lips opened and closed in the driving mirror, her teeth flashing, the tip of her tongue there for a moment. What she'd asked him was as clear as anyone would say it.

'We do of course,' he said, confusing St Teresa of Ávila with the St Teresa who'd been famous for her humility and her attention to little things. 'Grand,' Cahal said of her also. 'Grand altogether.'

To his disappointment, Spanish was spoken again. He was

going with Minnie Fennelly, but no doubt about it this woman had the better of her. The two faces appeared side by side in his mind's eye and there wasn't a competition. He drove past the cottages beyond the bridge, the road twisting and turning all over the place after that. It said earlier on the radio there'd be showers but there wasn't a trace of one, the October evening without a breeze, dusk beginning.

'Not more than a mile,' he said, not turning his head, but the Spanish was still going on. If they were planning to take photographs they mightn't be lucky by the time they got there. With the trees, Pouldearg was a dark place at the best of times. He wondered if the Germans had scored yet. He'd have put money on the Germans if he'd had any to spare.

Before they reached their destination Cahal drew the car on to the verge where it was wide and looked dry. He could tell from the steering that there was trouble and found it in the front offside wheel, the tyre leaking at the valve. Five or six pounds it would have lost, he estimated.

'It won't take me a minute,' he reassured his passengers, rummaging behind where they sat, among old newspapers and tools and empty paint tins, for the pump. He thought for a moment it mightn't be there and wondered what he'd do if the spare tyre was flat, which sometimes it was if a car was a trade-in. But the pump was there and he gave the partially deflated tyre a couple of extra pounds to keep it going. He'd see how things were when they reached Pouldearg crossroads.

When they did, there wasn't enough light for a photograph, but they went up close to the wayside Virgin, which was more lopsided than Cahal remembered it from the last time he'd driven by it, hardly longer than a year ago. The tyre had lost the extra pressure he'd pumped in and while they were occupied he began to change the wheel, having discovered that the spare tyre wasn't flat. All the time he could hear them talking in Spanish, although their voices weren't raised. When they returned to the car it was still jacked up and they had to wait for a while, standing on the road beside him, but they didn't appear to mind.

He'd still catch most of the second half, Cahal said to himself when eventually he turned the car and began the journey back. You never knew how you were placed as regards how long you'd be, how long you'd have to wait for people while they poked about.

'Was she all right for you?' he asked them, turning on the headlights so that the potholes would show up.

They answered in Spanish, as if they had forgotten that it wouldn't be any good. She'd fallen over a bit more, he said, but they didn't understand. They brought up the man they'd met in the public house in Dublin. They kept repeating something, a gabble of English words that still appeared to be about getting married. In the end, it seemed to Cahal that this man had told them people received a marriage blessing when they came to Pouldearg as penitents.

'Did you buy him drinks?' he asked, but that wasn't understood either.

They didn't meet another car, nor even a bicycle until they were further down. He'd been lucky over the tyre: they could easily have said they wouldn't pay if he'd had them stranded all night in the hills. They weren't talking any more; when he looked in the mirror they were kissing, no more than shadows in the gloom, arms around one another.

It was then, just after they'd passed the dead trees, that the child ran out. She came out of the blue cottage and ran at the car. He'd heard of it before, the child on this road who ran out at cars. It had never happened to himself, he'd never even seen a child there any time he'd passed, but often it was mentioned. He felt the thud no more than a second after the headlights picked out the white dress by the wall and then the sudden movement of the child running out.

Cahal didn't stop. In his mirror the road had gone dark again. He saw something white lying there but said to himself he had imagined it. In the back of the Cortina the embrace continued.

Sweat had broken on the palms of Cahal's hands, on his back and his forehead. She'd thrown herself at the side of the car and his own door was what she'd made contact with. Her mother was the unmarried woman of that cottage, many the time he'd heard that said in the garage. Fitzie Gill had shown him damage to his wing and said the child must have had a stone in her hand. But usually there wasn't any damage, and no one had ever mentioned damage to the child herself.

Bungalows announced the town, all of them lit up now. The Spanish began again, and he was asked if he could tell them what time the bus went to Galway. There was confusion because he thought they meant tonight, but then he understood it was the morning. He told them and when they paid him in Macey's yard the man handed him a pencil and a notebook. He didn't know what that was for, but they showed him, making gestures, and he wrote down the time of the bus. They shook hands with him before they went into the hotel.

In the very early morning, just after half past one, Cahal woke up and couldn't sleep again. He tried to recall what he'd seen of the football, the moves there'd been, the saves, the yellow card shown twice. But nothing seemed quite right, as if the television pictures and snatches of the commentary came from a dream, which he knew they hadn't. He had examined the side of the car in the garage and there'd been nothing. He had switched out the lights of the garage and locked up. He'd watched the football in Shannon's and hadn't seen the end because he lost interest when nothing much was happening. He should have stopped; he didn't know why he hadn't. He couldn't remember braking. He didn't know if he'd tried to, he didn't know if there hadn't been time.

The Ford Cortina had been seen setting out on the Loye road, and then returning. His father knew the way he'd gone, past the unmarried woman's cottage. The Spaniards would have said in the hotel they'd seen the Virgin. They'd have said in the hotel they were going on to Galway. They could be found in Galway for questioning.

In the dark Cahal tried to work it out. They would have heard the bump. They wouldn't have known what it was, but they'd have heard it while they were kissing one another. They would remember how much longer it was before they got out of the car in Macey's yard. It hadn't been a white dress, Cahal realized suddenly: it trailed on the ground, too long for a dress, more like a nightdress.

He'd seen the woman who lived there a few times when she came in to the shops, a dressmaker they said she was, small and wiry with dark inquisitive eyes and a twist in her features that made them less appealing than they might have been. When her child had been born to her the father had not been known – not even to herself, so it was said, though possibly without justification. People said she didn't speak about the birth of her child.

As Cahal lay in the darkness, he resisted the compulsion to get up in order to go back and see for himself; to walk out to the blue cottage, since to drive would be foolish; to look on the road for whatever might be there, he didn't know what. Often he and Minnie Fennelly got up in the middle of the night in order to meet in the back shed at her house. They lay on a stack of netting there, whispering and petting one another, the way they couldn't anywhere in the daytime. The best they could manage in the daytime was half an hour in the Ford Cortina out in the country somewhere. They could spend half the night in the shed.

He calculated how long it would take him to walk out to where the incident had occurred. He wanted to; he wanted to get there and see nothing on the road and to close his eyes in relief. Sometimes dawn had come by the time he parted from Minnie Fennelly, and he imagined that too, the light beginning as he walked in from the country feeling all right again. But more likely he wouldn't be.

'One day that kid'll be killed,' he heard Fitzie Gill saying, and someone else said the woman wasn't up to looking after the kid. The child was left alone in the house, people said, even for a night while the woman drank by herself in Leahy's, looking around for a man to keep her company.

That night, Cahal didn't sleep again. And all the next day he waited for someone to walk into the garage and say what had been found. But no one did, and no one did the next day either, or the day after that. The Spaniards would have gone on from Galway by now, the memories of people who had maybe noticed the Ford Cortina would be getting shaky. And Cahal counted the drivers whom he knew for a fact had experienced similar incidents with the child and said to himself that maybe, after all, he'd been fortunate. Even so, it would be a long time before he drove past that cottage again, if ever he did.

Then something happened that changed all that. Sitting with Minnie Fennelly in the Cyber Café one evening, Minnie Fennelly said, 'Don't look, only someone's staring at you.'

'Who is it?'

'D'you know that dressmaker woman?'

They'd ordered chips and they came just then. Cahal didn't say anything, but knew that sooner or later he wasn't going to be able to prevent himself from looking around. He wanted to ask if the woman had her child with her, but in the town he had only ever seen her on her own and he knew that the child wouldn't be there. If she was it would be a chance in a thousand, he thought, the apprehension that had haunted him on the night of the incident flooding his consciousness, stifling everything else.

'God, that one gives me the creeps!' Minnie Fennelly muttered, splashing vinegar on to her chips.

Cahal looked round them. He caught a glimpse of the dressmaker, alone, before he quickly looked back. He could still feel her eyes on his back. She would have been in Leahy's; the way she was sitting suggested drunkenness. When they'd finished their chips and the coffee they'd been brought while they were waiting, he asked if she was still there.

'She is all right. D'you know her? Does she come into the garage?'

'Ah no, she hasn't a car. She doesn't come in.'

'I'd best be getting back, Cahal.'

He didn't want to go yet, while the woman was there. But if they waited they could be here for hours. He didn't want to pass near her, but as soon as he'd paid and stood up he saw they'd have to. When they did she spoke to Minnie Fennelly, not him.

'Will I make your wedding-dress for you?' the dressmaker offered. 'Would you think of me at all when it'll be the time you'd want it?'

And Minnie Fennelly laughed and said no way they were ready for wedding-dresses yet.

'Cahal knows where he'll find me,' the dressmaker said. 'Amn't I right, Cahal?'

'I thought you didn't know her,' Minnie Fennelly said when they were outside.

*

Three days after that, Mr Durcan left his pre-war Riley in because the hand-brake was slipping. He'd come back for it at four, he arranged, and said before he left:

'Did you hear that about the dressmaker's child?'

He wasn't the kind to get things wrong. Fussy, with a thin black moustache, his Riley Sports the pride of his bachelor life, he was as tidy in what he said as he was in how he dressed.

'Gone missing,' he said now. 'The gardai are in on it.'

It was Cahal's father who was being told this. Cahal, with the cooling system from Gibney's bread van in pieces on a workbench, had just found where the tube had perished.

'She's backward, the child,' his father said.

'She is.'

'You hear tales.'

'She's gone off for herself anyway. They have a block on a couple of roads, asking was she seen.'

The unease that hadn't left him since the dressmaker had been in the Cyber Café began to nag again when Cahal heard that. He wondered what questions the gardai were asking; he wondered when it was that the child had taken herself off; although he tried, he couldn't piece anything together.

'Isn't she a backward woman herself though?' his father remarked when Mr Durcan had gone. 'Sure, did she ever lift a finger to tend that child?'

Cahal didn't say anything. He tried to think about marrying Minnie Fennelly, although still nothing was fixed, not even an agreement between themselves. Her plump honest features became vivid for a moment in his consciousness, the same plumpness in her arms and her hands. He found it attractive, he always had, since first he'd noticed her when she was still going to the nuns. He shouldn't have had thoughts about the Spanish girl, he shouldn't have let himself. He should have told them the statue was nothing, that the man they'd met had been pulling a fast one for the sake of the drinks they'd buy him.

'Your mother had that one run up curtains for the back room,' his father said. 'Would you remember that, boy?'

Cahal shook his head.

'Ah, you wouldn't have been five at the time, maybe younger yet. She was just after setting up with the dressmaking, her father still there in the cottage with her. The priests said give her work on account she was a charity. Bedad, they wouldn't say it now!'

Cahal turned the radio on and turned the volume up. Madonna was singing, and he imagined her in the get-up she'd fancied for herself a few years ago, suspenders and items of underclothes. He'd thought she was great.

'I'm taking the Toyota out,' his father said, and the bell from the forecourt rang, someone waiting there for petrol. It didn't concern him, Cahal told himself as he went to answer it. What had occurred on the evening of Germany and Holland was a different thing altogether from the news Mr Durcan had brought, no way could it be related.

'Howya,' he greeted the school-bus driver at the pumps.

The dressmaker's child was found where she'd lain for several days, at the bottom of a fissure, half covered with shale, in the exhausted quarry half a mile from where she'd lived. Years ago the last of the stone had been carted away and a barbed-wire fence put up, with two warning notices about danger. She would have crawled in under the bottom strand of wire, the gardai said, and a chain-link fence replaced the barbed wire within a day.

In the town the dressmaker was condemned, blamed behind her back for the tragedy that had occurred. That her own father, who had raised her on his own since her mother's early death, had himself been the father of the child was an ugly calumny, not voiced before, but seeming now to have a natural place in the paltry existence of a child who had lived and died wretchedly.

'How are you, Cahal?' Cahal heard the voice of the dressmaker behind him when, early one November morning, he made his way to the shed where he and Minnie Fennelly indulged their affection for one another. It was not yet one o'clock, the town lights long ago extinguished except for a few in Main Street. 'Would you come home with me, Cahal? Would we walk out to where I am?'

All this was spoken to his back while Cahal walked on. He knew who was there. He knew who it was, he didn't have to look.

'Leave me alone,' he said.

'Many's the night I rest myself on the river seat and many's the night I see you. You'd always be in a hurry, Cahal.'

'I'm in a hurry now.'

'One o'clock in the morning! Arrah, go on with you, Cahal!'

'I don't know you. I don't want to be talking to you.'

'She was gone for five days before I went to the Guards. It wouldn't be the first time she was gone off. A minute wouldn't go by without she was out on the road.'

Cahal didn't say anything. Even though he still didn't turn round he could smell the drink on her, stale and acrid.

'I didn't go to them any quicker for fear they'd track down the way it was when the lead would be fresh for them. D'you understand me, Cahal?'

Cahal stopped. He turned round and she almost walked into him. He told her to go away.

'The road was the thing with her. First thing of a morning she'd be running at the cars without a pick of food inside her. The next thing is she'd be off up the road to the statue. She'd kneel to the statue the whole day until she was found by some old fellow who'd bring her back to me. Some old fellow'd have her by the hand and they'd walk in the door. Oh, many's the time, Cahal. Wasn't it the first place the Guards looked when I said that to the Sergeant? Any woman'd do her best for her own, Cahal.'

'Will you leave me alone!'

'Gone seven it was, maybe twenty past. I had the door open to go in to Leahy's and I seen the black car going by and yourself inside it. You always notice a car in the evening time, only the next thing was I was late back from Leahy's and she was gone. D'you understand me, Cahal?'

'It's nothing to do with me.'

'He'd have gone back the same way he went out, I said to myself, but I didn't mention it to the Guards, Cahal. Was she in the way of wandering in her nightdress? was what they asked me and I told them she'd be out the door before you'd see her. Will we go home, Cahal?'

'I'm not going anywhere with you.'

'There'd never be a word of blame on yourself, Cahal.'

'There's nothing to blame me for. I had people in the car that evening.'

'I swear before God, what's happened is done with. Come back with me now, Cahal.'

'Nothing happened, nothing's done with. There was Spanish people in the car the entire time. I drove them out to Pouldearg and back again to Macey's Hotel.'

'Minnie Fennelly's no use to you, Cahal.'

He had never seen the dressmaker close before. She was younger than he'd thought, but still looked a fair bit older than himself, maybe twelve or thirteen years. The twist in her face wasn't ugly, but it spoilt what might have been beauty of a kind, and he remembered the flawless beauty of the Spanish girl and the silkiness of her hair. The dressmaker's hair was black too, but wild and matted, limply straggling, falling to her shoulders. The eyes that had stared so intensely at him in the Cyber Café were bleary. Her full lips were drawn back in a smile, one of her teeth slightly chipped. Cahal walked away and she did not follow him.

That was the beginning; there was no end. In the town, though never again at night, she was always there: Cahal knew that was an illusion, that she wasn't always there but seemed so because her presence on each occasion meant so much. She tidied herself up; she wore dark clothes, which people said were in mourning for her child; and people said she had ceased to frequent Leahy's public house. She was seen painting the front of her cottage, the same blue shade, and tending its bedraggled front garden. She walked from the shops of the town, and never now stood, hand raised, in search of a lift.

Continuing his familiar daily routine of repairs and servicing and answering the petrol bell, Cahal found himself unable to dismiss the connection between them that the dressmaker had made him aware of when she'd walked behind him in the night, and knew that the roots it came from spread and gathered strength and were nurtured, in himself, by fear. Cahal was afraid without knowing what he was afraid of, and when he tried to work this out he was bewildered. He began to go to mass and to confession more often than he ever had before. It was noticed by his father that he had even less to say these days to the customers at the pumps or when they left their cars in. His mother wondered about his being anaemic and put him on iron pills. Returning occasionally to the town for a couple of days at a weekend, his sister who was still in Ireland said the trouble must surely be to do with Minnie Fennelly.

During all this time – passing in other ways quite normally – the child was lifted again and again from the cleft in the rocks, still in her nightdress as Cahal had seen her, laid out and wrapped as the dead are wrapped. If he hadn't had to change the wheel he would have passed the cottage at a different time and the chances were she wouldn't have been ready to run out, wouldn't just then have felt inclined to. If he'd explained to the Spaniards about the Virgin's tears being no more than rain he wouldn't have been on the road at all.

The dressmaker did not speak to him again or seek to, but he knew that the fresh blue paint, and the mourning clothes that were not, with time, abandoned, and the flowers that came to fill the small front garden, were all for him. When a little more than a year had passed since the evening he'd driven the Spanish couple out to Pouldearg, he attended Minnie Fennelly's wedding when she married Des Downey, a vet from Athenry.

The dressmaker had not said it, but it was what there had been between them in the darkened streets: that he had gone back, walking out as he had wanted to that night when he'd lain awake, that her child had been there where she had fallen on the road, that he had carried her to the quarry. And Cahal knew it was the dressmaker, not he, who had done that.

He visited the Virgin of the Wayside, always expecting that she might be there. He knelt, and asked for nothing. He spoke only in his thoughts, offering reparation and promising to accept whatever might be visited upon him for associating himself with the mockery of the man the Spaniards had met by chance in Dublin, for mocking the lopsided image on the road, taking fifty euros for a lie. He had looked at them kissing. He had thought about Madonna with her clothes off, not minding that she called herself that.

Once when he was at Pouldearg, Cahal noticed the glisten

of what had once been taken for tears on the Virgin's cheek. He touched the hollow where this moisture had accumulated and raised his dampened finger to his lips. It did not taste of salt, but that made no difference. Driving back, when he went by the dressmaker's blue cottage, she was there in the front garden, weeding her flowerbeds. Even though she didn't look up, he wanted to go to her and knew that one day he would.

The Hill Bachelors

In the kitchen of the farmhouse she wondered what they'd do about her, what they'd suggest. It was up to them; she couldn't ask. It wouldn't be seemly to ask, it wouldn't feel right.

She was a small woman, spare and wiry, her mourning clothes becoming her. At sixty-eight she had ailments: arthritis in her knuckles and her ankles, though only slightly a nuisance to her; a cataract she was not yet aware of. She had given birth without much difficulty to five children, and was a grandmother to nine. Born herself far from the hills that were her home now, she had come to this house forty-seven years ago, had shared its kitchen and the rearing of geese and hens with her husband's mother, until the kitchen and the rearing became entirely her own. She hadn't thought she would be left. She hadn't wanted it. She didn't now.

He walked into the hills from where the bus had dropped him on the main road, by Caslin's petrol pumps and shop across the road from the Master McGrath Bar and Lounge, owned by the Caslins also. It was midday and it was fine. After four hours in two different buses he welcomed the walk and the fresh air. He had dressed himself for the funeral so that he wouldn't have to bring the extra clothes in a suitcase he'd have had to borrow. Overnight necessities were in a ragged blue shopping bag which, every working day, accompanied him in the cab of the lorry he drove, delivering sacks of flour to the premises of bakers, and cartons of pre-packed bags to retailers.

Everything was familiar to him: the narrow road, in need of repair for as long as he had known it, the slope rising gently at first, the hills in the far distance becoming mountains, fields and conifers giving way to marsh and a growth that couldn't be identified from where he walked but which he knew was fern, then heather and bog cotton with here and there a patch of grass. Not far below the skyline were the corrie lakes he had never seen.

He was a dark-haired young man of twenty-nine, slightly made, pink cheeks and a certain chubbiness about his features giving him a genial, easygoing air. He was untroubled as he walked on, reflecting only that a drink and a packet of potato crisps at the Master McGrath might have been a good idea. He wondered how Maureen Caslin had turned out; when they were both fifteen he'd thought the world of her.

At a crossroads he turned to the left, on to an unmade-up boreen, scarcely more than a track. Around him there was a silence he remembered also, quite different from the kind of silence he had become used to in or around the midland towns for which, eleven years ago, he had left these hills. It was broken when he had walked another mile by no more than what seemed like a vibration in the air, a faint disturbance that might have been, at some great distance, the throb of an aeroplane. Five minutes later, rust-eaten and muddy, a front wing replaced but not yet painted, Hartigan's old red Toyota clattered over the potholes and the tractor tracks. The two men waved to each other and then the ramshackle car stopped.

'How're you, Paulie?' Hartigan said.

'I'm all right, Mr Hartigan. How're you doing yourself?'

Hartigan said he'd been better. He leaned across to open the passenger door. He said he was sorry, and Paulie knew what he meant. He had wondered if he'd be in luck, if

Hartigan would be coming back from Drunbeg this midday. A small, florid man, Hartigan lived higher up in the hills with a sister who was more than a foot taller than he was, a lean, gangling woman who liked to be known only as Miss Hartigan. On the boreen there were no other houses.

'They'll be coming back?' Hartigan enquired above the rasping noise of the Toyota's engine, referring to Paulie's two brothers and two sisters.

'Ah, they will surely.'

'He was out in the big field on the Tuesday.'

Paulie nodded. Hartigan drove slowly. It wasn't a time for conversation, and that was observed.

'Thanks, Mr Hartigan,' Paulie said as they parted, and waved when the Toyota drove on. The sheepdogs barked at him and he patted their heads, recognizing the older one. The yard was tidy. Hartigan hadn't said he'd been down lending a hand but Paulie could tell he had. The back door was open, his mother expecting him.

'It's good you came back,' she said.

He shook his head, realizing as soon as he had made it that the gesture was too slight for her to have noticed. He couldn't not have come back. 'How're you doing?' he said.

'All right. All right.'

They were in the kitchen. His father was upstairs. The others would come and then the coffin would be closed and his father would be taken to the church. That was how she wanted it: the way it always was when death was taken from the house.

'It was never good between you,' she said.

'I'd come all the same.'

Nothing was different in the kitchen: the same green paint, worn away to the timber at two corners of the dresser and around the latch of the doors that led to the yard and to the stairs; the same delft seeming no more chipped or cracked on the dresser shelves, the big scrubbed table, the clutter on the smoky mantel-shelf above the stove, the uncomfortable chairs, the flagged floor, the receipts on the spike in the window.

'Sit with him a while, Paulie.'

His father had always called him Paul, and he was called Paul in his employment, among the people of the midland towns. Paul was what Patsy Finucane called him.

'Go up to him, Paulie. God rest him,' she said, a plea in her tone that bygones should be bygones, that the past should be misted away now that death had come, that prayer for the safe delivery of a soul was what mattered more.

'Will they all come together?' he asked, still sitting there. 'Did they say that?'

'They'll be here by three. Kevin's car and one Aidan'll hire.'

He stood up, his chair scraping on the flagstones. He had asked the questions in order to delay going up to his father's bedside. But it was what she wanted, and what she was saying without saying it was that it was what his father wanted also. There would be forgiveness in the bedroom, his own spoken in a mumble, his father's taken for granted.

He took the rosary she held out to him, not wishing to cause offence.

Hearing his footsteps on the brief, steeply pitched stairs, hearing the bedroom door open and close, the footsteps again in the room above her, then silence, she saw now what her returned son saw: the bloodless pallor, the stubble that had come, eyelids drawn, lips set, the grey hair she had combed. Frances had been the favourite, then Mena; Kevin was approved of because he was reliable; Aidan was the first-born. Paulie hadn't been often mentioned.

There was the sound of a car, far back on the boreen. A while it would take to arrive at the farmhouse. She set out cups and saucers on the table, not hurrying. The kettle had boiled earlier and she pushed it back on to the hot plate of the stove. Not since they were children had they all been back at the same time. There wouldn't be room for them for the two nights they'd have to spend, but they'd have their own ideas about how to manage that. She opened the back door so that there'd be a welcome.

Paulie looked down at the stretched body, not trusting himself to address it in any way. Then he heard the cars arriving and crossed the room to the window. In the yard Frances was getting out of one and the other was being backed so that it wouldn't be in the way, a white Ford he'd never seen before. The window was open at the top and he could hear the voices, Kevin saying it hadn't been a bad drive at all and Aidan agreeing. The Ford was hired, *Cahill of Limerick* it said on a sticker; picked up at Shannon it would have been.

The husbands of Paulie's sisters hadn't come, maybe because of the shortage of sleeping space. They'd be looking after the Dublin children, and it seemed that Kevin's Sharon had stayed behind with theirs in Carlow. Aidan had come on his own from Boston. Paulie had never met Aidan's wife and Sharon only once; he'd never met any of the children. They could have managed in a single car, he calculated, watching his brothers and sisters lifting out their suitcases, but it might have been difficult to organize, Kevin having to drive round by Shannon.

His brothers wore black ties, his sisters were in mourning of a kind, not entirely, because that could wait till later. Mena looked pregnant again. Kevin had a bald patch now. Aidan took off the glasses he had worn to drive. Their suitcases weren't heavy. You could tell there was no intention to stay longer than was necessary.

Looking down into the yard, Paulie knew that an assumption had already been made, as he had known it in the kitchen when he sat there with his mother. He was the bachelor of the family, the employment he had wasn't much. His mother couldn't manage on her own.

He had known it in Meagher's back bar when he told Patsy Finucane he had a funeral to go to. The death had lost him Patsy Finucane: it was her, not his father, he thought about when he heard of it, and in Meagher's the stout ran away with him and he spoke too soon. 'Jeez,' she said, 'what would I do in a farmhouse!'

Afterwards – when the journey through the hills had become a funeral procession at the edge of the town, when the coffin had been delivered to its night's resting place, and later when the burial was complete and the family had returned to the farmhouse and had dispersed the next morning – Paulie remained.

He had not intended to. He had hoped to get a lift in one of the two cars, and then to take a bus, and another bus, as he had on his journey over.

'Where is it they'll separate?' his mother asked in the quietness that followed the departure.

He didn't know. Somewhere that was convenient; in some town they would pull in and have a drink, different now that they weren't in a house of mourning. They would exchange news it hadn't seemed right to exchange before. Aidan would talk about Boston, offering his sisters and his brother hospitality there.

'Warm yourself at the fire, Paulie.'

'Wait till I see to the heifers first.'

'His boots are there.'

'I know.'

His brothers had borrowed the gum boots, too; wherever you went, you needed them. Kevin had fixed a fence, Aidan had got the water going again in the pipe up to the sheep. Between them, they'd taken the slack out of the barbed wire beyond the turf bog.

'Put on a waterproof, Paulie.'

It wasn't going to rain, but the waterproof kept the wind out. Whenever he remembered the farmhouse from his childhood it was windy – the fertilizer bags blowing about in the yard, blustery on the track up to the sheep hills, in the big field that had been the family's mainstay ever since his father had cleared the rocks from it, in the potato field. Wind, more than rain or frost, characterized the place, not that there wasn't a lot of rain too. But who'd mind the rain? his father used to say.

The heifers didn't need seeing to, as he had known they wouldn't. They stood, miserably crouched in against the wall of a fallen barn, mud that the wind had dried hanging from them. His father had taken off the roof when one of the other walls had collapsed, needing the corrugated iron for somewhere else. He'd left the standing wall for the purpose the heifers put it to now.

Paulie, too, stood in the shelter of the wall, the puddles at his feet not yet blown dry, as the mud had on the animals. He remembered the red roof lifted down, piece by piece, Kevin waiting below to receive it, Aidan wrenching out the bolts. He had backed the tractor, easing the trailer close to where they were. 'What's he want it for?' he'd asked Kevin, and Kevin said the corrugated iron would be used for filling the gaps in the hedges.

Slowly, Paulie walked back the way he had come. 'D'you

think of coming back?' Aidan had said, saying it in the yard when they were alone. Paulie had known it would be said and had guessed it would be Aidan who'd say it, Aidan being the oldest. 'I'm only mentioning it,' Aidan had said. 'I'm only touching on it.'

Blowing at the turf with the wheel-bellows, she watched the glow spread, sparks rising and falling away. It hadn't been the time to make arrangements or even to talk about them. Nothing could have been more out of place, and she was glad they realized that. Kevin had had a word with Hartigan after the funeral, something temporary fixed up, she could tell from the gestures.

They'd write. Frances had said she would, and Aidan had. Sharon would write for Kevin, as she always did. Mena would. Wherever it was they stopped to say goodbye to one another they'd talk about it and later on they'd write.

'Sit down, Paulie, sit down,' she said when her son came in, bringing the cold with him.

She said again that Father Kinally had done it beautifully. She'd said so yesterday to her daughters in the car, she'd said it to Kevin and to Aidan this morning. Paulie would have heard, yet you'd want to repeat it. You felt the better for it.

'Ah, he did,' Paulie said. 'He did of course.'

He'd taken over. She could feel he'd taken over, the way he'd gone out to see were the heifers all right, the way it was he who remembered, last evening and this morning, that there was the bit of milking to do, that he'd done it without a word. She watched him ease off the gum boots and set them down by the door. He hung the waterproof on the door hook that was there for it and came to the fire in his socks, with his shoes in one hand. She turned away so that he wouldn't notice she'd been reminded of his father coming into the kitchen also.

'Aren't the heifers looking good?' she said.

'Oh, they are, they are.'

'He was pleased with them this year.'

'They're not bad, all right.'

'Nothing's fetching at the minute, all the same.'

He nodded. He naturally would know times were bad, neither sheep nor cattle fetching what they were a year ago, everything gone quiet, the way you'd never have believed it.

'We're in for the night so,' she said.

'We are.'

She washed the eggs Mena had collected earlier, brushing off the marks on them, then wiped the shells clean before she piled them in the bowl. The eggs would keep them going, with the rashers left over and half a saucepan of stew in the fridge. 'You've enough for an army!' Kevin had said, looking into the deep-freeze, and she reminded him you had to have enough in case the weather came in bad.

'What'd we do without it?' she said now, mentioning the deep-freeze. They'd had half a pig from the Caslins, only a portion of the belly used up so far. 'And mutton till Doomsday,' she said.

'How're they these days, the Caslins? I didn't notice Maureen at the funeral.'

'Maureen married a man in Tralee. She's there since.'

'Who's the man?'

'He's in a shoe shop.'

They could have gone to the wedding only it had been a period of the year when you wouldn't want to spare the time. The Hartigans had gone. They'd have taken her but she'd said no.

'Hartigan came back drunk, you should have seen the cut of him! And herself with a frost on her that would have quenched the fire!'

'He's driving down in the morning. He'll pick me up.'

Rashers and black pudding and fried bread were ready on the pan. She cracked two eggs into the fat, turned them when they were ready because he liked them turned. When she placed the plate in front of him he took a mouthful of tea before he ate anything. He said:

'You couldn't manage. No way.'

'It wasn't a time to talk about it, Paulie.'

'I'll come back.'

He began to eat, the yolk of the eggs spreading yellow on the plate. He left the black pudding and the crisp fat of the bacon until last. He'd always done that.

'Hartigan'd still come down. I'm all right on the bit of milking. I'm all right on most things. The Caslins would come up.'

'You couldn't live like that.'

'They're neighbours, Paulie. They got help from himself if they wanted it. I looked over and saw Kevin having a word with Hartigan in the graveyard. It won't be something for nothing, not with Hartigan. Kevin'll tell me later.'

'You'd be dependent.'

'You have your own life, Paulie.'

'You have what there is.'

He ate for several minutes in silence, then he finished the tea that had been poured for him.

'I'd have to give in notice. I'd have to work the notice out. A month.'

'Think it over before you'll do anything, Paulie.'

Paulie harboured no resentment, not being a person who easily did: going back to the farmhouse was not the end of the world. The end of the world had been to hear, in Meagher's back bar, that life on a farm did not attract Patsy Finucane.

As soon as he'd mentioned marriage that day he knew he shouldn't have. Patsy Finucane had taken fright like a little young greyhound would. She'd hardly heard him when he said, not knowing what else to say, 'Ah well, no matter.' It was a nervousness mixed in with the stout that had caused him to make the suggestion, and as soon as he had there was no regaining her: before she looked away that was there in her soft grey eyes. 'I won't go back so,' he'd said, making matters worse. 'I won't go back without you.'

When they sat again in Meagher's back bar after the funeral Paulie tried to put things right; he tried to begin again, but it wasn't any good. During the third week of his working out his notice Patsy Finucane began to go out with a clerk from the post office.

In the yard she threw down grains for the hens and remembered doing it for the first time, apprehensive then about what she'd married into. Nor had her apprehension been misplaced: more than she'd imagined, her position in the household was one of obedience and humility, and sometimes what was said, or incidents that occurred, left a sting that in private drew tears from her. Yet time, simply in passing, transformed what seemed to be immutable. Old age enfeebled on the one hand; on the other, motherhood nurtured confidence. In the farmhouse, roles were reversed.

She didn't want distress like that for any wife Paulie would eventually bring to the kitchen and the house. She would make it easier, taking a back seat from the start and be glad to do so. It was only a pity that Maureen Caslin had married the shoe-shop man, for Maureen Caslin would have suited him well. There were the sisters, of course.

During the weeks that followed Paulie's departure, the anticipated letters came from Mena and Frances and from her daughter-in-law Sharon on behalf of Kevin, and from Aidan. The accumulated content was simple, the unstated expectation stated at last, four times over in different handwriting. Aidan said he and Paulie had had a talk about it. *You are good to think of me*, she wrote back, four times also.

Hartigan continued to come down regularly and a couple of times his sister accompanied him, sitting in the kitchen while he saw to any heavy work in the yard. 'Would Mena have room for you?' she enquired on one of these occasions, appearing to forget that Paulie was due to return when he'd worked out his notice. Miss Hartigan always brought sultana bread when she came and they had it with butter on it. 'I only mentioned Mena,' she said, 'in case Paulie wouldn't be keen to come back. I was thinking he maybe wouldn't.'

'Why's that, Miss Hartigan?'

'It's bachelors that's in the hills now. Like himself,' Miss Hartigan added, jerking her bony head in the direction of the yard, where her brother was up on a ladder, fixing a gutter support.

'Paulie's not married either, though.'

'That's what I'm saying to you. What I'm saying is would he want to stop that way?'

Miss Hartigan's features were enriched by a keenness to say more, to inform and explain, to dispel the bewilderment she had caused. She did so after a pause, politely reaching for a slice of sultana bread. It might not have been noticed that these days the bachelors of the hills found it difficult to attract a wife to the modest farms they inherited.

'Excuse me for mentioning it,' Miss Hartigan apologized before she left.

It was true, and it had been noticed and often remarked upon. Hartigan himself, twenty years ago, was maybe the first of the hill bachelors: by now you could count them – lone men, some of them kept company by a mother or a sister – on the slopes of Coumpeebra, on Slievenacoush, on Knockrea, on Luirc, on Clydagh.

She didn't remember putting all that from her mind when Paulie had said he would come back, but perhaps she had. She tried not to think about it, comforting herself that what had been said, and the tone of Miss Hartigan's voice, had more to do with Miss Hartigan and her brother than with the future in a neighbouring farmhouse. Nor did it necessarily need to be that what had already happened would continue to happen. The Hartigans' stretch of land was worse by a long way than the land lower down on the hill; no better than the side of Slievenacoush, or Clydagh or Coumpeebra. You did the best you could, you hoped for warm summers. Paulie was a good-looking, decent boy; there was no reason at all why he wouldn't bring up a family here as his father had.

'There's two suitcases left down with the Caslins,' he said when he walked in one Saturday afternoon. 'When I get the car started I'll go down for them.'

They didn't embrace; there'd never been much of that in the family. He sat down and she made tea and put the pan on. He told her about the journey, how a woman had been singing on the first of the two buses, how he'd fallen asleep on the second. He was serious the way he told things, his expression intent, sometimes not smiling much. He'd always been like that.

'Hartigan started the car a while back,' she said, 'to make sure it was in form.'

'And it was? All right?'

'Oh, it was, it was.'

'I'll take a look at it later.'

He settled in easily, and she realized as he did so that she had never known him well. He had been lost to her in the family, his shadowy place in it influenced by his father's lack of interest in him. She had never protested about that, only occasionally whispering a surreptitious word or two of comfort. It was fitting in a way that a twist of fate had made him his father's inheritor.

As if he had never been away, he went about his daily tasks knowledgeably and efficiently. He had forgotten nothing – about the winter feed for the heifers, about the work around the yard or where the fences might give way on the hills or how often to go up there after the sheep, about keeping the tractor right. It seemed, which she had not suspected before, that while his presence was so often overlooked he had watched his father at work more conscientiously than his brothers had. 'He'd be proud of you these days,' she said once, but Paulie did not acknowledge that and she resisted making the remark again. The big field, which had been his father's pride, became his. There was another strip to the south of it that could be cleared and reclaimed, he said, and he took her out to show her where he would run the new wall. They stood in the sunshine on a warm June morning while he pointed and talked about it, the two sheepdogs obedient by him. He was as good with them as his father ever had been.

He drove her, as his father had, every three weeks down to Drunbeg, since she had never learned to drive herself. His father used to wait in the car park of Conlon's Supermarket while she shopped, but Paulie always went in with her. He pushed the trolley and sometimes she gave him a list and he added items from the shelves. 'Would we go and see that?' he suggested one time when they were passing the Two-Screen Rialto, which used to be just the Picture House before it was given a face-lift. She wouldn't be bothered, she said.

She'd never been inside the cinema, either in the old days or since it had become a two-screen; the television was enough for her. 'Wouldn't you take one of the Caslin girls?' she said.

He took the older of them, Aileen, and often after that he drove down in the evenings to sit with her in the Master McGrath. The relationship came to an end when Aileen announced that her sister in Tralee had heard of a vacancy in a newsagent and confectioner's, that she'd been to Tralee herself to be looked over and in fact had been offered the position.

'And did you know she had intentions that way?' Paulie's mother asked him when she heard, and he said he had, in a way. He didn't seem put about, although she had assumed herself that by the look of things Aileen Caslin – stolid and on the slow side – would be the wife who'd come to the farmhouse, since her sister Maureen was no longer available. Paulie didn't talk about it, but quite soon after Aileen's departure he began to take an interest in a girl at one of the payouts in Conlon's.

'Wouldn't you bring Maeve out one Sunday?' his mother suggested when the friendship had advanced, when there'd been visits to the two-screen and evenings spent together drinking, as there'd been with Aileen Caslin. Maeve was a fair bit livelier than Aileen; he could do worse.

But Maeve never came to the farmhouse. In Conlon's Paulie took to steering the trolley to one of the other payouts even when the queue at hers was shorter. His mother didn't ask why. He had his own life, she kept reminding herself; he had his privacy, and why shouldn't he? 'Isn't he the good boy to you?' Father Kinally remarked one Sunday after Mass when Paulie was turning the car. 'Isn't it grand the way it's turned out for you?'

She knew it was and gratefully gave thanks for it. Being more energetic than his father had been at the end, Paulie worked a longer day, far into the evening when it was light enough.

'I don't know did I ever speak a word to her,' she said when he began to go out with the remaining Caslin daughter. Sensible, she looked.

'Ah, sure, anything,' the youngest of the three Caslin girls always said when Paulie told her what films were on and asked which she'd like to see. When the lights went down he waited a bit before he put an arm around her, as he always had with her sisters and with Maeve. He hadn't been able to wait with Patsy Finucane.

The sensible look that Paulie's mother had noted in Annie Caslin was expressed in a matter-of-fact manner. Sentiment played little part in her stalwart, steady nature. She was the tallest and in a general way the biggest of the three Caslin girls, with black hair that she curled and distinctive features that challenged one another for dominance – the slightly large nose, the wide mouth, the unblinking gaze. Paulie took her out half a dozen times before she confessed that what she wanted to do was to live in a town. She'd had the roadside Master McGrath, she said; she'd had serving petrol at the pumps. 'God, I don't know how you'd stand it up in the bogs,' she said before Paulie had a chance to ask her if she'd be interested in coming up to the farmhouse. Even Drunbeg would do her, she said, and got work six months later in the fertilizer factory.

Paulie asked other girls to go out with him, but by then it had become known that what he was after was marriage. One after another, they made excuses, a fact that Hartigan was aware of when he pulled up the Toyota one morning beside a gateway where Paulie was driving in posts. He didn't say anything, but often Hartigan didn't.

'Will it rain, Mr Hartigan?' Paulie asked him.

'The first time I saw your mammy,' Hartigan said, rejecting a discussion about the weather, 'she was stretching out sheets on the bushes. Six years of age I was, out after a hare.'

'A while ago, all right.'

'Amn't I saying it to you?'

Not understanding the conversation, Paulie vaguely shook his head. He struck the post he was easing into the ground another blow. Hartigan said:

'I'd take the big field off you.'

'Ah no, no.'

That was why he had stopped. It might even have been that he'd driven down specially when he heard the thud of the sledgehammer on the posts, saying to himself that it was a good time for a conversation.

'I wouldn't want to sell the field, Mr Hartigan.'

'But wouldn't you do well all the same if you did? Is it a life at all for a young fellow?'

Paulie didn't say anything. He felt the post to see if it was steady yet. He struck it again, three times before he was satisfied.

'You need a bit of company, boy,' Hartigan said before he backed into the gateway and drove up the hill again.

What she had succeeded in keeping at bay since Miss Hartigan had spoken of it was no longer possible to evade. When Paulie told her about Patsy Finucane she was pleased that he did, glad that he didn't keep it to himself. She knew about everything else: it was all of a piece that Hartigan was trying to get the land cheap by taking advantage of the same circumstances that had left him a bachelor himself. Who could blame him? she said to herself, but even so she wondered if Paulie – so agreeable and good-hearted – would become like that in his time; if he'd become hard, as his father had been, and as grasping as Hartigan.

'I'll go to Mena,' she said. 'There's room there.'

'Ah, there isn't.'

'They'd fit me in.'

'It's here there's room.'

'You want to be married, Paulie. Any man does.'

'He'd take a day shifting a boulder with the tractor. He'd put a ditch through the marsh to gain another half yard. He never minded how long a thing took.'

'It's now we're talking about, Paulie.'

'There'd be sheep in this house within a twelvemonth if Hartigan had it, the doors taken off and made use of, and the next thing is the wind'd be shifting the slates. There'd be grazing taken out of the big field until there wasn't a blade of grass left standing. The marsh'd come in again. No one'd lift a finger.'

'You didn't know what you were coming back to.'

'Ah, I did. I did.'

Obligingly, he lied. You'd say to yourself he was easygoing. When he'd told her about the Finucane girl he'd said it was the way things were. No matter, he'd said. Often you'd forget he wasn't easygoing at all; often she did.

'There's no need, Paulie.'

'There is.'

He said it quietly, the two words hanging there after he had spoken, and she realized that although it was her widowhood that had brought him back it wasn't her widowhood that made him now insist he must remain. She could argue for ever and he would not go now.

'You're good, Paulie,' she said, since there was nothing else left to say.

He shook his head, his dark hair flopping from side to side. 'Arrah, no.'

'You are. You are, Paulie.'

When her own death came, her other children would return, again all at the same time. The coffin would be carried down the steep stairs, out into the van in the yard, and the funeral would go through the streets of Drunbeg, and the next day there'd be the Mass. They'd go away then, leaving Paulie in the farmhouse.

'Wait till I show you,' he said, and he took her out to where he was draining another half yard. He showed her how he was doing it. He showed her the temporary wall he had put up, sheets of red corrugated that had come from the old shed years ago.

'That's great,' she said. 'Great, Paulie.'

A mist was coming in off the hills, soft and gentle, the clouds darkening above it. The high edge of Slievenacoush was lost. Somewhere over the boglands a curlew cried.

'Go in out of the drizzle,' he said, when they had stood there for a few minutes.

'Don't stay out long yourself, Paulie.'

Guilt was misplaced, goodness hardly came into it. Her widowing and the mood of a capricious time were not of consequence, no more than a flicker in a scheme of things that had always been there. Enduring, unchanging, the hills had waited for him, claiming one of their own.

The Piano Tuner's Wives

Violet married the piano tuner when he was a young man. Belle married him when he was old.

There was a little more to it than that, because in choosing Violet to be his wife the piano tuner had rejected Belle, which was something everyone remembered when the second wedding was announced. 'Well, she got the ruins of him anyway,' a farmer of the neighbourhood remarked, speaking without vindictiveness, stating a fact as he saw it. Others saw it similarly, though most of them would have put the matter differently.

The piano tuner's hair was white and one of his knees became more arthritic with each damp winter that passed. He had once been svelte but was no longer so, and he was blinder than on the day he married Violet – a Thursday in 1951, June 7th. The shadows he lived among now had less shape and less density than those of 1951.

'I will,' he responded in the small Protestant church of St Colman, standing almost exactly as he had stood on that other afternoon. And Belle, in her fifty-ninth year, repeated the words her one-time rival had spoken before this altar also. A decent interval had elapsed; no one in the church considered that the memory of Violet had not been honoured, that her passing had not been distressfully mourned. '. . . and with all my worldly goods I thee endow,' the piano tuner stated, while his new wife thought she would like to be standing beside him in white instead of suitable wine-red. She had not attended the first wedding, although she had been invited.

She'd kept herself occupied that day, whitewashing the chicken shed, but even so she'd wept. And tears or not, she was more beautiful – and younger by almost five years – than the bride who so vividly occupied her thoughts as she battled with her jealousy. Yet he had preferred Violet – or the prospect of the house that would one day become hers, Belle told herself bitterly in the chicken shed, and the little bit of money there was, an easement in a blind man's existence. How understandable, she was reminded later on, whenever she saw Violet guiding him as they walked, whenever she thought of Violet making everything work for him, giving him a life. Well, so could she have.

As they left the church the music was by Bach, the organ played by someone else today, for usually it was his task. Groups formed in the small graveyard that was scattered around the small grey building, where the piano tuner's father and mother were buried, with ancestors on his father's side from previous generations. There would be tea and a few drinks for any of the wedding guests who cared to make the journey to the house, two miles away, but some said goodbye now, wishing the pair happiness. The piano tuner shook hands that were familiar to him, seeing in his mental eye faces that his first wife had described for him. It was the depth of summer, as in 1951, the sun warm on his forehead and his cheeks, and on his body through the heavy wedding clothes. All his life he had known this graveyard, had first felt the letters on the stones as a child, spelling out to his mother the names of his father's family. He and Violet had not had children themselves, though they'd have liked them. He was her child, it had been said, a statement that was an irritation for Belle whenever she heard it. She would have given him children, of that she felt certain.

'I'm due to visit you next month,' the old bridegroom

reminded a woman whose hand still lay in his, the owner of a Steinway, the only one among all the pianos he tuned. She played it beautifully. He asked her to whenever he tuned it, assuring her that to hear was fee enough. But she always insisted on paying what was owing.

'Monday the third I think it is.'

'Yes, it is, Julia.'

She called him Mr Dromgould: he had a way about him that did not encourage familiarity in others. Often when people spoke of him he was referred to as the piano tuner, this reminder of his profession reflecting the respect accorded to the possessor of a gift. Owen Francis Dromgould his full name was.

'Well, we had a good day for it,' the new young clergyman of the parish remarked. 'They said maybe showers but sure they got it wrong.'

'The sky –?'

'Oh, cloudless, Mr Dromgould, cloudless.'

'Well, that's nice. And you'll come on over to the house, I hope?'

'He must, of course,' Belle pressed, then hurried through the gathering in the graveyard to reiterate the invitation, for she was determined to have a party.

Some time later, when the new marriage had settled into a routine, people wondered if the piano tuner would begin to think about retiring. With a bad knee, and being sightless in old age, he would readily have been forgiven in the houses and the convents and the school halls where he applied his skill. Leisure was his due, the good fortune of company as his years slipped by no more than he deserved. But when, occasionally, this was put to him by the loquacious or the inquisitive he denied that anything of the kind was in his thoughts, that he considered only the visitation of death as bringing any kind of end. The truth was, he would be lost without his work, without his travelling about, his arrival every six months or so in one of the small towns to which he had offered his services for so long. No, no, he promised, they'd still see the white Vauxhall turning in at a farm gate or parked for half an hour in a convent play-yard, or drawn up on a verge while he ate his lunchtime sandwiches, his tea poured out of a Thermos by his wife.

It was Violet who had brought most of this activity about. When they married he was still living with his mother in the gate-lodge of Barnagorm House. He had begun to tune pianos – the two in Barnagorm House, another in the town of Barnagorm, and one in a farmhouse he walked to four miles away. In those days he was a charity because he was blind, was now and again asked to repair the sea-grass seats of stools or chairs, which was an ability he had acquired, or to play at some function or other the violin his mother had bought him in his childhood. But when Violet married him she changed his life. She moved into the gate-lodge, she and his mother not always agreeing but managing to live together none the less. She possessed a car, which meant she could drive him to wherever she discovered a piano, usually long neglected. She drove to houses as far away as forty miles. She fixed his charges, taking the consumption of petrol and wear and tear to the car into account. Efficiently, she kept an address book and marked in a diary the date of each next tuning. She recorded a considerable improvement in earnings, and saw that there was more to be made from the playing of the violin than had hitherto been realized: Country-and-Western evenings in lonely public houses, the crossroads platform dances of summer – a practice that in 1951 had not entirely died out. Owen Dromgould delighted in his violin and would play it anywhere, for profit or not. But Violet was keen on the profit.

So the first marriage busily progressed, and when eventually Violet inherited her father's house she took her husband to live there. Once a farmhouse, it was no longer so, the possession of the land that gave it this title having long ago been lost through the fondness for strong drink that for generations had dogged the family but had not reached Violet herself.

'Now, tell me what's there,' her husband requested often in their early years, and Violet told him about the house she had brought him to, remotely situated on the edge of the mountains that were blue in certain lights, standing back a bit from a bend in a lane. She described the nooks in the rooms, the wooden window shutters he could hear her pulling over and latching when wind from the east caused a draught that disturbed the fire in the room once called the parlour. She described the pattern of the carpet on the single flight of stairs, the blue-and-white porcelain knobs of the kitchen cupboards, the front door that was never opened. He loved to listen. His mother, who had never entirely come to terms with his affliction, had been impatient. His father, a stableman at Barnagorm House who'd died after a fall, he had never known. 'Lean as a greyhound,' Violet described his father from a photograph that remained.

She conjured up the big, cold hall of Barnagorm House. 'What we walk around on the way to the stairs is a table with a peacock on it. An enormous silvery bird with bits of coloured glass set in the splay of its wings to represent the splendour of the feathers. Greens and blues,' she said when he asked the colour, and yes, she was certain it was only glass, not jewels, because once, when he was doing his best with the badly flawed grand in the drawing-room, she had been told that. The stairs were on a curve, he knew from going up and down them so often to the Chappell in the nursery. The first landing was dark as a tunnel, Violet said, with two sofas, one at each end, and rows of unsmiling portraits half lost in the shadows of the walls.

'We're passing Doocey's now,' Violet would say. 'Father Feely's getting petrol at the pumps.' Esso it was at Doocey's, and he knew how the word was written because he'd asked and had been told. Two different colours were employed; the shape of the design had been compared with shapes he could feel. He saw, through Violet's eyes, the gaunt façade of the McKirdys' house on the outskirts of Oghill. He saw the pallid face of the stationer in Kiliath. He saw his mother's eyes closed in death, her hands crossed on her breast. He saw the mountains, blue on some days, misted away to grey on others. 'A primrose isn't flamboyant,' Violet said. 'More like straw or country butter, with a spot of colour in the middle.' And he would nod, and know. Soft blue like smoke, she said about the mountains; the spot in the middle more orange than red. He knew no more about smoke than what she had told him also, but he could tell those sounds. He knew what red was, he insisted, because of the sound; orange because you could taste it. He could see red in the Esso sign and the orange spot in the primrose. 'Straw' and 'country butter' helped him, and when Violet called Mr Whitten gnarled it was enough. A certain Mother Superior was austere. Anna Craigie was fanciful about the eyes. Thomas in the sawmills was a streel. Bat Conlon had the forehead of the Merricks' retriever, which was stroked every time the Merricks' Broadwood was attended to.

Between one woman and the next, the piano tuner had managed without anyone, fetched by the possessors of pianos and driven to their houses, assisted in his shopping and his housekeeping. He felt he had become a nuisance to people, and knew that Violet would not have wanted that. Nor would she have wanted the business she built up for him to be neglected because she was no longer there. She was proud that he played the organ in St Colman's Church. 'Don't ever stop doing that,' she whispered some time before she whispered her last few words, and so he went alone to the church. It was on a Sunday, when two years almost had passed, that the romance with Belle began.

Since the time of her rejection Belle had been unable to shake off her jealousy, resentful because she had looks and Violet hadn't, bitter because it seemed to her that the punishment of blindness was a punishment for her too. For what else but a punishment could you call the dark the sightless lived in? And what else but a punishment was it that darkness should be thrown over her beauty? Yet there had been no sin to punish and they would have been a handsome couple, she and Owen Dromgould. An act of grace it would have been, her beauty given to a man who did not know that it was there.

It was because her misfortune did not cease to nag at her that Belle remained unmarried. She assisted her father first and then her brother in the family shop, making out tickets for the clocks and watches that were left in for repair, noting the details for the engraving of sports trophies. She served behind the single counter, the Christmas season her busy time, glassware and weather indicators the most popular wedding gifts, cigarette lighters and inexpensive jewellery for lesser occasions. In time, clocks and watches required only the fitting of a battery, and so the gift side of the business was expanded. But while that time passed there was no man in the town who lived up to the one who had been taken from her.

Belle had been born above the shop, and when house and shop became her brother's she continued to live there. Her brother's children were born, but there was still room for her, and her position in the shop itself was not usurped. It was she who kept the chickens at the back, who always had been in charge of them, given the responsibility on her tenth birthday: that, too, continued. That she lived with a disappointment had long ago become part of her, had made her what she was for her nieces and her nephew. It was in her eyes, some people noted, even lent her beauty a quality that enhanced it. When the romance began with the man who had once rejected her, her brother and his wife considered she was making a mistake, but did not say so, only laughingly asked if she intended taking the chickens with her.

That Sunday they stood talking in the graveyard when the handful of other parishioners had gone. 'Come and I'll show you the graves,' he said, and led the way, knowing exactly where he was going, stepping on to the grass and feeling the first gravestone with his fingers. His grandmother, he said, on his father's side, and for a moment Belle wanted to feel the incised letters herself instead of looking at them. They both knew, as they moved among the graves, that the parishioners who'd gone home were very much aware of the two who had been left behind. On Sundays, ever since Violet's death, he had walked to and from his house, unless it happened to be raining, in which case the man who drove old Mrs Purtill to church took him home also. 'Would you like a walk, Belle?' he asked when he had shown her his family graves. She said she would.

Belle didn't take the chickens with her when she became a wife. She said she'd had enough of chickens. Afterwards she regretted that, because every time she did anything in the house that had been Violet's she felt it had been done by Violet before her. When she cut up meat for a stew, standing with the light falling on the board that Violet had used, and on the knife, she felt herself a follower. She diced carrots, hoping that Violet had sliced them. She bought new wooden spoons because Violet's had shrivelled away so. She painted the upright rails of the banisters. She painted the inside of the front door that was never opened. She disposed of the stacks of women's magazines, years old, that she found in an upstairs cupboard. She threw away a frying-pan because she considered it unhygienic. She ordered new vinyl for the kitchen floor. But she kept the flowerbeds at the back weeded in case anyone coming to the house might say she was letting the place become run-down.

There was always this dichotomy: what to keep up, what to change. Was she giving in to Violet when she tended her flowerbeds? Was she giving in to pettiness when she threw away a frying-pan and three wooden spoons? Whatever Belle did she afterwards doubted herself. The dumpy figure of Violet, grey-haired as she had been in the end, her eyes gone small in the plumpness of her face, seemed irritatingly to command. And the unseeing husband they shared, softly playing his violin in one room or another, did not know that his first wife had dressed badly, did not know she had thickened and become sloppy, did not know she had been an unclean cook. That Belle was the one who was alive, that she was offered all a man's affection, that she plundered his other woman's possessions and occupied her bedroom and drove her car, should have been enough. It should have been everything, but as time went on it seemed to Belle to be scarcely anything at all. He had become set in ways that had been allowed and hallowed in a marriage of nearly forty years: that was what was always there.

A year after the wedding, as the couple sat one lunchtime in the car which Belle had drawn into the gateway to a field, he said:

'You'd tell me if it was too much for you?'

'Too much, Owen?'

'Driving all over the county. Having to get me in and out. Having to sit there listening.'

'It's not too much.'

'You're good the way you've patience.'

'I don't think I'm good at all.'

'I knew you were in church that Sunday. I could smell the perfume you had on. Even at the organ I could smell it.'

'I'll never forget that Sunday.'

'I loved you when you let me show you the graves.'

'I loved you before that.'

'I don't want to tire you out, with all the traipsing about after pianos. I could let it go, you know.'

He would do that for her, her thought was as he spoke. He wasn't much for a woman, he had said another time: a blind man moving on towards the end of his days. He confessed that when first he wanted to marry her he hadn't put it to her for more than two months, knowing better than she what she'd be letting herself in for if she said yes. 'What's that Belle look like these days?' he had asked Violet a few years ago, and Violet hadn't answered at first. Then apparently she'd said: 'Belle still looks a girl.'

'I wouldn't want you to stop your work. Not ever, Owen.'

'You're all heart, my love. Don't say you're not good.'

'It gets me out and about too, you know. More than ever in my life. Down all those avenues to houses I didn't know were there. Towns I've never been to. People I never knew. It was restricted before.'

The word slipped out, but it didn't matter. He did not reply that he understood about restriction, for that was not his style. When they were getting to know one another, after that Sunday by the church, he said he'd often thought of her in her brother's jeweller's shop, wrapping up what was purchased there, as she had wrapped for him the watch he bought for one of Violet's birthdays. He'd thought of her putting up the grilles over the windows in the evenings and locking the shop door, and then going upstairs to sit with her brother's family. When they were married she told him more: how most of the days of her life had been spent, only her chickens her own. 'Smart in her clothes,' Violet had added when she said the woman he'd rejected still looked a girl.

There hadn't been any kind of honeymoon, but a few months after he had wondered if travelling about was too much for her he took Belle away to a seaside resort where he and Violet had many times spent a week. They stayed in the same boarding-house, the Sans Souci, and walked on the long, empty strand and in lanes where larks scuttered in and out of the fuchsia, and on the cliffs. They drank in Malley's public house. They lay in autumn sunshine on the dunes.

'You're good to have thought of it.' Belle smiled at him, pleased because he wanted her to be happy.

'Set us up for the winter, Belle.'

She knew it wasn't easy for him. They had come to this place because he knew no other; he was aware before they set out of the complication that might develop in his emotions when they arrived. She had seen that in his face, a stoicism that was there for her. Privately, he bore the guilt of betrayal, stirred up by the smell of the sea and seaweed. The voices in the boarding-house were the voices Violet had heard. For Violet, too, the scent of honeysuckle had lingered into October. It was Violet who first said a week in the autumn sun would set them up for the winter: that showed in him, also, a moment after he spoke the words.

'I'll tell you what we'll do,' he said. 'When we're back we'll get you the television, Belle.'

'Oh, but you –'

'You'd tell me.'

They were walking near the lighthouse on the cape when he said that. He would have offered the television to Violet, but Violet must have said she wouldn't be bothered with the thing. It would never be turned on, she had probably argued; you only got silliness on it anyway.

'You're good to me,' Belle said instead.

'Ah no, no.'

When they were close enough to the lighthouse he called out and a man called back from a window. 'Hold on a minute,' the man said, and by the time he opened the door he must have guessed that the wife he'd known had died. 'You'll take a drop?' he offered when they were inside, when the death and the remarriage had been mentioned. Whiskey was poured, and Belle felt that the three glasses lifted in salutation were an honouring of her, although this was not said. It rained on the way back to the boarding-house, the last evening of the holiday.

'Nice for the winter,' he said as she drove the next day through rain that didn't cease. 'The television.'

When it came, it was installed in the small room that once was called the parlour, next to the kitchen. This was where mostly they sat, where the radio was. A fortnight after the arrival of the television set Belle acquired a small black sheepdog that a farmer didn't want because it was afraid of sheep. This dog became hers and was always called hers. She fed it and looked after it. She got it used to travelling with them in the car. She gave it a new name, Maggie, which it answered to in time.

But even with the dog and the television, with additions and disposals in the house, with being so sincerely assured that she was loved, with being told she was good, nothing changed for Belle. The woman who for so long had taken her husband's arm, who had guided him into rooms of houses where he coaxed pianos back to life, still claimed existence. Not as a tiresome ghost, some unforgiving spectre uncertainly there, but as if some part of her had been left in the man she'd loved.

Sensitive in ways that other people weren't, Owen Dromgould continued to sense his second wife's unease. She knew he did. It was why he had offered to give up his work, why he'd taken her to Violet's seashore and borne there the guilt of his betrayal, why there was a television set now, and a sheepdog. He had guessed why she'd re-covered the kitchen floor. Proudly, he had raised his glass to her in the company of a man who had known Violet. Proudly, he had sat with her in the dining-room of the boarding-house and in Malley's public house.

Belle made herself remember all that. She made herself see the bottle of John Jameson taken from a cupboard in the lighthouse, and hear the boarding-house voices. He understood, he did his best to comfort her; his affection was in everything he did. But Violet would have told him which leaves were on the turn. Violet would have reported that the tide was going out or coming in. Too late Belle realized that. Violet had been his blind man's vision. Violet had left her no room to breathe.

One day, coming away from the house that was the most distant they visited, the first time Belle had been there, he said:

'Did you ever see a room as sombre as that one? Is it the holy pictures that do it?'

Belle backed the car and straightened it, then edged it

through a gateway that, thirty years ago, hadn't been made wide enough.

'Sombre?' she said on a lane like a riverbed, steering around the potholes as best she could.

'We used wonder could it be they didn't want anything colourful in the way of a wallpaper in case it wasn't respectful to the pictures.'

Belle didn't comment on that. She eased the Vauxhall out on to the tarred road and drove in silence over a stretch of bogland. Vividly she saw the holy pictures in the room where Mrs Grenaghan's piano was: Virgin and Child, Sacred Heart, St Catherine with her lily, the Virgin on her own, Jesus in glory. They hung against nondescript brown; there were statues on the mantelpiece and on a corner shelf. Mrs Grenaghan had brought tea and biscuits to that small, melancholy room, speaking in a hushed tone as if the holiness demanded that.

'What pictures?' Belle asked, not turning her head, although she might have, for there was no other traffic and the bog road was straight.

'Aren't the pictures still in there? Holy pictures all over the place?'

'They must have taken them down.'

'What's there then?'

Belle went a little faster. She said a fox had come from nowhere, over to the left. It was standing still, she said, the way foxes do.

'You want to pull up and watch him, Belle?'

'No. No, he's moved on now. Was it Mrs Grenaghan's daughter who played that piano?'

'Oh, it was. And she hasn't seen that girl in years. We used say the holy pictures maybe drove her away. What's on the walls now?'

'A striped paper.' And Belle added: 'There's a photograph of the daughter on the mantelpiece.'

Some time later, on another day, when he referred to one of the sisters at the convent in Meena as having cheeks as flushed as an eating apple, Belle said that that nun was chalky white these days, her face pulled down and sunken. 'She has an illness so,' he said.

Suddenly more confident, not caring what people thought, Belle rooted out Violet's plants from the flowerbeds at the back, and grassed the flowerbeds over. She told her husband of a change at Doocey's garage: Texaco sold instead of Esso. She described the Texaco logo, the big red star and how the letters of the word were arranged. She avoided stopping at Doocey's in case a conversation took place there, in case Doocey were asked if Esso had let him down, or what. 'Well, no, I wouldn't call it silvery exactly,' Belle said about the peacock in the hall of Barnagorm House. 'If they cleaned it up I'd say it's brass underneath.' Upstairs, the sofas at each end of the landing had new loose covers, bunches of different-coloured chrysanthemums on them. 'Well no, not *lean*, I wouldn't call him that,' Belle said with the photograph of her husband's father in her hand. 'A sturdy face, I'd say.' A schoolteacher whose teeth were once described as gusty had false teeth now, less of a mouthful, her smile sedate. Time had apparently drenched the bright white of the McKirdys' façade, almost a grey you'd call it. 'Forget-me-not blue,' Belle said one day, speaking of the mountains that were blue when the weather brought that colour out. 'You'd hardly credit it.' And it was never again said in the piano tuner's house that the blue of the mountains was the subtle blue of smoke.

Owen Dromgould had run his fingers over the bark of trees. He could tell the difference in the outline of their leaves; he could tell the thorns of gorse and bramble. He knew birds from their song, dogs from their bark, cats from the touch of them on his legs. There were the letters on the gravestones, the stops of the organ, his violin. He could see red, berries on holly and cotoneaster. He could smell lavender and thyme.

All that could not be taken from him. And it didn't matter if, overnight, the colour had worn off the kitchen knobs. It didn't matter if the china light-shade in the kitchen had a crack he hadn't heard about before. What mattered was damage done to something as fragile as a dream.

The wife he had first chosen had dressed drably: from silence and inflexions – more than from words – he learned that now. Her grey hair straggled to her shoulders, her back was a little humped. He poked his way about, and they were two old people when they went out on their rounds, older than they were in their ageless happiness. She wouldn't have hurt a fly, she wasn't a person you could be jealous of, yet of course it was hard on a new wife to be haunted by happiness, to be challenged by the simplicities there had been. He had given himself to two women; he hadn't withdrawn himself from the first, he didn't from the second.

Each house that contained a piano brought forth its contradictions. The pearls old Mrs Purtill wore were opals, the pallid skin of the stationer in Kiliath was freckled, the two lines of oaks above Oghill were surely beeches? 'Of course, of course,' Owen Dromgould agreed, since it was fair that he should do so. Belle could not be blamed for making her claim, and claims could not be made without damage or destruction. Belle would win in the end because the living always do. And that seemed fair also, since Violet had won in the beginning and had had the better years.

POCKET PENGUINS

1. Lady Chatterley's Trial
2. **Eric Schlosser** Cogs in the Great Machine
3. **Nick Hornby** Otherwise Pandemonium
4. **Albert Camus** Summer in Algiers
5. **P. D. James** Innocent House
6. **Richard Dawkins** The View from Mount Improbable
7. **India Knight** On Shopping
8. **Marian Keyes** Nothing Bad Ever Happens in Tiffany's
9. **Jorge Luis Borges** The Mirror of Ink
10. **Roald Dahl** A Taste of the Unexpected
11. **Jonathan Safran Foer** The Unabridged Pocketbook of Lightning
12. **Homer** The Cave of the Cyclops
13. **Paul Theroux** Two Stars
14. **Elizabeth David** Of Pageants and Picnics
15. **Anaïs Nin** Artists and Models
16. **Antony Beevor** Christmas at Stalingrad
17. **Gustave Flaubert** The Desert and the Dancing Girls
18. **Anne Frank** The Secret Annexe
19. **James Kelman** Where I Was
20. **Hari Kunzru** Noise
21. **Simon Schama** The Bastille Falls
22. **William Trevor** The Dressmaker's Child
23. **George Orwell** In Defence of English Cooking
24. **Michael Moore** Idiot Nation
25. **Helen Dunmore** Rose, 1944
26. **J. K. Galbraith** The Economics of Innocent Fraud
27. **Gervase Phinn** The School Inspector Calls
28. **W. G. Sebald** Young Austerlitz
29. **Redmond O'Hanlon** Borneo and the Poet
30. **Ali Smith** Ali Smith's Supersonic 70s
31. **Sigmund Freud** Forgetting Things
32. **Simon Armitage** King Arthur in the East Riding
33. **Hunter S. Thompson** Happy Birthday, Jack Nicholson
34. **Vladimir Nabokov** Cloud, Castle, Lake
35. **Niall Ferguson** 1914: Why the World Went to War

POCKET PENGUINS

36. **Muriel Spark** The Snobs
37. **Steven Pinker** Hotheads
38. **Tony Harrison** Under the Clock
39. **John Updike** Three Trips
40. **Will Self** Design Faults in the Volvo 760 Turbo
41. **H. G. Wells** The Country of the Blind
42. **Noam Chomsky** Doctrines and Visions
43. **Jamie Oliver** Something for the Weekend
44. **Virginia Woolf** Street Haunting
45. **Zadie Smith** Martha and Hanwell
46. **John Mortimer** The Scales of Justice
47. **F. Scott Fitzgerald** The Diamond as Big as the Ritz
48. **Roger McGough** The State of Poetry
49. **Ian Kershaw** Death in the Bunker
50. **Gabriel García Márquez** Seventeen Poisoned Englishmen
51. **Steven Runciman** The Assault on Jerusalem
52. **Sue Townsend** The Queen in Hell Close
53. **Primo Levi** Iron Potassium Nickel
54. **Alistair Cooke** Letters from Four Seasons
55. **William Boyd** Protobiography
56. **Robert Graves** Caligula
57. **Melissa Bank** The Worst Thing a Suburban Girl Could Imagine
58. **Truman Capote** My Side of the Matter
59. **David Lodge** Scenes of Academic Life
60. **Anton Chekhov** The Kiss
61. **Claire Tomalin** Young Bysshe
62. **David Cannadine** The Aristocratic Adventurer
63. **P. G. Wodehouse** Jeeves and the Impending Doom
64. **Franz Kafka** The Great Wall of China
65. **Dave Eggers** Short Short Stories
66. **Evelyn Waugh** The Coronation of Haile Selassie
67. **Pat Barker** War Talk
68. **Jonathan Coe** 9th & 13th
69. **John Steinbeck** Murder
70. **Alain de Botton** On Seeing and Noticing

In 1935 if you wanted to read a good book, you needed either a lot of money or a library card. Cheap paperbacks were available, but their poor production generally mirrored the quality between the covers. One weekend that year, Allen Lane, Managing Director of The Bodley Head, having spent the weekend visiting Agatha Christie, found himself on a platform at Exeter station trying to find something to read for his journey back to London. He was appalled by the quality of the material he had to choose from. Everything that Allen Lane achieved from that day until his death in 1970 was based on a passionate belief in the existence of 'a vast reading public for *intelligent* books at a low price'. The result of his momentous vision was the birth not only of Penguin, but of the 'paperback revolution'. Quality writing became available for the price of a packet of cigarettes, literature became a mass medium for the first time, a nation of book-borrowers became a nation of book-buyers – and the very concept of book publishing was changed for ever. Those founding principles – of quality and value, with an overarching belief in the fundamental importance of reading – have guided everything the company has done since 1935. Sir Allen Lane's pioneering spirit is still very much alive at Penguin in 2005. Here's to the next 70 years!

MORE THAN A BUSINESS

'We decided it was time to end the almost customary half-hearted manner in which cheap editions were produced – as though the only people who could possibly want cheap editions must belong to a lower order of intelligence. We, however, believed in the existence in this country of a vast reading public for intelligent books at a low price, and staked everything on it'
Sir Allen Lane, 1902–1970

'The Penguin Books are splendid value for sixpence, so splendid that if other publishers had any sense they would combine against them and suppress them'
George Orwell

'More than a business … a national cultural asset'
Guardian

'When you look at the whole Penguin achievement you know that it constitutes, in action, one of the more democratic successes of our recent social history'
Richard Hoggart